"MINE WILL," SAID JOHN

by Helen V. Griffith
pictures by Jos. A. Smith

Greenwillow Books, New York

jE

Watercolor paints, colored pencils, and watercolor
pencils were used for the full-color art.
The text type is Icone No. 55

Text copyright © 1980 by Helen V. Griffith
Illustrations copyright © 1992 by Jos. A. Smith
First published in 1980 by Greenwillow Books.
New edition, with new illustrations, published in 1992
by Greenwillow Books.   All rights reserved.
No part of this book may be reproduced or utilized
in any form or by any means, electronic or mechanical,
including photocopying, recording, or by any information
storage and retrieval system, without permission
in writing from the Publisher, Greenwillow Books,
a division of William Morrow & Company, Inc.,
1350 Avenue of the Americas, New York, NY 10019.

Printed in Singapore by Tien Wah Press
First Edition   10 9 8 7 6 5 4 3 2 1

Library of Congress Cataloging-in-Publication Data
Griffith, Helen V.
"Mine will," said John / by Helen V. Griffith ;
pictures by Jos. A. Smith.
p.   cm.
Summary: John's parents try to interest him
in a gerbil or chameleon or frog for a pet, but
John will be content only with a puppy.
ISBN 0-688-10957-8 (trade).
ISBN 0-688-10958-6 (lib)
[1. Pets—Fiction.]
I. Smith, Joseph A. (Joseph Anthony) (date), ill.
II. Title.   PZ7.G8823Mi   1992
[E]—dc20   91-32476   CIP   AC

*F*or my parents
and, of course, John
—H. V. G.

*F*or Kari, Joe, and Emily,
and also Smaug,
Benji, Jenny, Tony, and Ilsa,
and all the snakes
who never were named
—J. A. S.

John and his parents were at the pet shop.
They were buying a pet for John.

"I would like a puppy," said John.
"Puppies are noisy," said his mother. "That is
why we are buying you this nice gerbil."

"Gerbils are noisy, too," said John. "They cry at night."

"Gerbils don't make any noise at all," his father said.

"Mine will," said John.

That night John put the gerbil in a box by his bed.
He climbed into bed and turned off the light.

The gerbil began to whimper.
Then the gerbil began to yelp.
It yelped and yelped.

John's parents came into the room.

"Did we hear something?" asked John's mother.

"The gerbil," said John.

They all looked at the gerbil.

It was curled up and sound asleep.

"It keeps me awake," said John.

John's parents looked at John.

Then they looked at each other.

The next day they took the gerbil back to the pet shop.

"It makes too much noise," John said.

"Gerbils don't make noise," said the pet shop owner.

"Mine did," said John.

They exchanged the gerbil for a chameleon.
"A chameleon will be nice and quiet," said
John's mother.

"Chameleons glow in the dark," said John. "They turn blue and pink and orange and purple."
"Chameleons turn green and brown, that's all," said John's father. "They don't glow in the dark."
"Mine will," said John.

That night John put the chameleon in a box
by his bed.
He climbed into bed and turned off the light.

The chameleon began to glow.
It turned blue and pink and orange and purple.

The whole room began to glow.

John put the chameleon under his blanket,
but the colors glowed through it—
purple and orange and pink and blue.

John's parents came into the room.

"Did we see something?" asked John's father.

"The chameleon," said John.

They all looked at the chameleon.

It was lying on its back, sound asleep.

"It keeps me awake," said John.

John's parents looked at John.

Then they looked at each other.

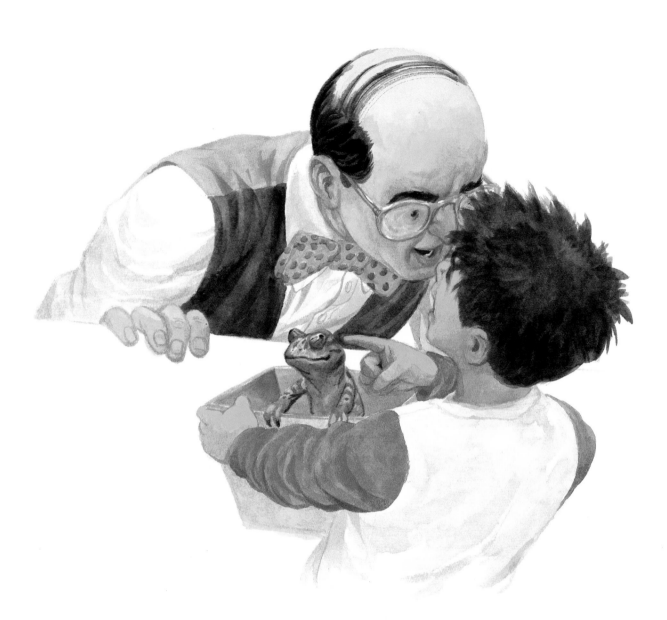

At the pet shop the next day John said,
"My chameleon glowed in the dark."
"Chameleons don't glow in the dark,"
 said the pet shop owner.
"Mine did," said John.

"I think we will exchange the chameleon for
a frog," said John's mother.
"Would you like a pet frog, John?"

"Frogs chew on furniture," said John.

"They chew all night long."

"Frogs don't have teeth," said John's father.

"They can't chew anything."

"Mine will," said John.

John's parents looked at each other.

Then they looked at John.

"John," said his father,
"pick out a puppy."

"Oh, good," said John. "I want this one."
"He won't cry at night and he won't glow
in the dark and he won't chew furniture.
He will always mind me, and he will love me
better than anything."

"Now, John," said his mother. "I don't think any puppy can be that good."

"Mine will," said John....

And it was.

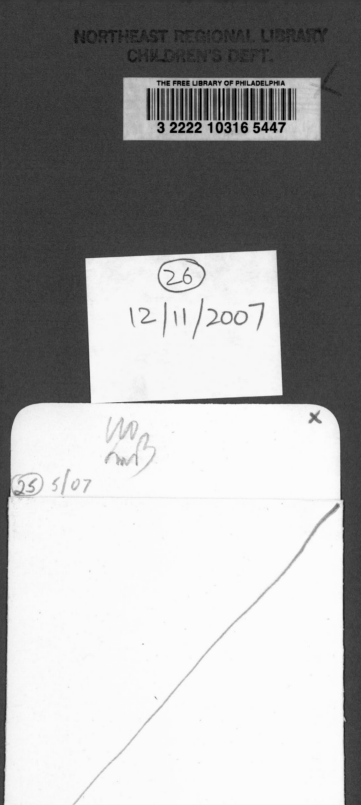